Frebie Dog Tales

The New Mailman, The Dog Catcher, and The Judge
Inspired by a true story

Dedicated to Everyman's Dog
In memory of Frebie and
In honor of his master, Doug

by Betty Reese Freberg
Painted by Leoma Lovegrove

Special thanks to my grandson,
Brian Bostwick,
for his expertise, love and support
in helping to make this book a reality.

Published by Freberg Publishing
P. O. Box 472
Azle, TX 76098
frebiedogtales@gmail.com

Text copyright ©2014 by Betty Reeese Freberg
Paintings copyright ©2014 by Leoma Lovegrove

ISBN-13: 978-1533151476
ISBN-10: 1533151474

My
Name
is
Frebie

FOR HANK
ARF ARF ARF

Love Always
Leoma Lovegrove

I like to jump fences and run free.

I live with Mimi in a town
where there is a "leash law."
This means I am not allowed to leave the
house or yard unless I am on a leash.

Mimi bought a harness
connected to a long leash for me
to wear in the back yard.
Sometimes I wiggle out of it
when she isn't looking and jump
the fence to go play
with my friends.

Then, I start
r-u-n-n-i-n-g.

I don't like to be a bad dog
or break the "leash law"
but I have a lot of friends
in my town who play with me.

I have a human friend who likes to
chase me with a long pole.

I call him **The Dog Catcher.**

We play hide-n-seek.
When he calls me,
I run and hide.
He never catches me.
Mimi and **The Dog Catcher**
are friends too.

One of my friends is the man who
brings our mail everyday.
I call him **The Mailman.**

One day I looked over the fence and saw a man
I didn't recognize coming towards my house.
He was in a uniform, carrying a bag
just like my friend, **The Mailman.**
I thought, "Is he **The <u>New</u> Mailman?**"

I wanted to tell him hello.
I wiggled out of my harness,
jumped over the fence and ran up to him
real fast with my tail wagging.

"Ouch!" Suddenly, I felt my eyes burning.
I couldn't see. I stumbled.

I tried to get my bearings.
My animal instincts clicked in.
I knew I had to get back home!
I used my smelling abilities
to sniff my way to the house.

I started barking,
"Mimi, Mimi, let me in!"
No answer.
Where was she? I was frantic!

Finally, the door flung open.

As I ran past **Mimi** up the stairs,
I heard her say,
"**Frebie**, what in the world is wrong with you?"

LEOMA
LOVEGROV

I hid under the bed!
I was scared!
I listened.
What had I done wrong?

I was only trying to be friendly.
I didn't bark at him.
I had my ears up with my tail wagging
just like **Mimi** had taught me to do
so people would know I was a good dog.

Now my eyes burned.
I laid very quietly,
listening and waiting.

Then, I heard **Mimi** calling me.

I crept down stairs
and crawled up on the den couch.
Mimi began to scold me from the doorway.

"Frebie, I know you like to run free.
But, you have to learn that with freedom
comes responsibilities.
Sometimes there are consequences
when you break rules and regulations!"

I listened as **Mimi** scolded me.
She used a lot of big words I didn't understand.
I didn't even care.

At that moment
I didn't want to run free.
I felt safe.

After the episode with **The New Mailman**,
I stayed in the yard or the house
for the next few days.

Then, one day I heard **Mimi** talking
to a man at the front door.
He said he had a
"Warrant of Arrest for a Vicious Dog."
Mimi sounded surprised,
"I have to go to court?
I didn't know dogs could be arrested."

There was only one dog in our house
and it was me.
What did "being arrested" mean?
It didn't sound good.

On the day **Mimi** had to go to court she said to me,
"No way am I putting you out in the yard
so you can jump and run.
You are staying in the house!"

Mimi was gone a long time.
I tried to calm my nerves.
I walked around the house.
I looked out of the windows.
I barked at a cat running up a tree.
Nothing seemed to help.
I was worried.

Mimi always forbid me to lay on our living room sofa.
She said it was for special occasions.
I felt today was special
and I needed a place to worry.
So, I curled up on the "forbidden" sofa.

Suddenly, I was startled awake when I heard **Mimi** talking on the phone about our day in court.

A man, called **The Judge**, asked **The New Mailman** what had happened. He said I was a very vicious dog. So, to protect himself, he sprayed me in the face with pepper spray. He wanted me arrested and put in the Dog Pound.

The Judge asked **The Dog Catcher** what he thought about me.
He said I was a friendly but elusive dog that would playfully hide and run from him.

This is true.

He is one of my favorite human friends.

Mimi told **The Judge**
she had never known me to be mean
and certainly not vicious.

The Judge said,
"This dog was breaking the law by running free.
He did evade **The Dog Catcher**
and did frighten **The New Mailman**.
This dog must be kept on a leash.

However, this dog did not bark, growl or jump on
The New Mailman".
And, **The Judge** added,
"I find it especially difficult to believe
this dog is vicious with a name like **Frebie**."

Case Dismissed!

Now **Mimi** takes me for walks on a leash everyday.
Sometimes she takes me out to the country
and lets me run free with the wind in my face.

I love **Mimi**, my home and my friends.
I know there are times in my life when
I have to follow some rules that I may not like.
Mimi says that is part of growing up.

But, in my heart, I'll always want to
jump, run and be free.

That's why —

My
Name
is
Frebie

The End...

Until the next **Frebie Dog Tales**

Note to young reader:

Do you have a pet you would like to write about?
Or, perhaps you have a "pretend" story you'd like to tell.
Or maybe you're an artist like, Leoma Lovegrove.
Would you like to put a book together?

Well, I want to encourage you to give it a try. As my mother used to say, "Nothing ventured, nothing gained." In other words if you don't try, you will never know what you can do.

I am eighty-five years old. Most people said, "Betty, you are too old to write a children's book. You can't do it." But, you know what? I did do it! I had lots of help, but I got it done. My family and friends were very encouraging.

You can too! Don't hesitate to ask for help. Think about the story you want to tell and just begin writing or creating. You will have to make a lot of corrections and work very hard, but you can make it happen. Give it a try!

Good luck. Happy writing and creating!

Your friend,

Betty Freberg (or just call me, "Mimi.")

Please let me hear from you:
frebiedogtales@gmail.com

Betty Reese Freberg is a Christian speaker, teacher, film maker and author. "Frebie Dog Tales" is her first children's book. Frebie came to live with Mimi (Betty) after his master and her son, Doug, had to move to the big city of Washington, DC. Betty is a widow, mother of seven grown children and grandmother of ten. She is author of the book "Ten Women of God" and founder of *The Tenth Woman* ministry. Betty enjoys traveling with her ministry and visiting with her family and friends. She is a lifelong Texan.

Leoma Lovegrove is known worldwide for her art work. "Frebie Dog Tales" is her first children's book. Leoma is a graduate of Ringling School of Art in Sarasota, FL. She is well known for her "Painting Out Loud" performances where she paints in front of live audiences. Portraits of Jimmy Carter, George W. Bush, and Richard Branson hang in respective locations throughout the US and England. She is famous for her "Beatle" series, coconut postcards and Bealls' Florida collection. she travels to Europe each year to recharge her artistic batteries but she and her husband, Michael Silberg, always return home to Matlacha, FL where they own and operate *Lovegrove Gallery and Gardens.*

Frebie was a mixture of Chow and German Shepard. He won the heart of his master, Doug, as a six week old puppy while Doug was a student at Baylor University. A thirteen year love relationship began between two free spirited beings. When Doug moved to Washington, DC, he asked his widowed mother, Mimi, to let Frebie live with her. Neither of them, Frebie nor Mimi, knew the adventures which were about to begin!

53867516R00020

Made in the USA
Lexington, KY
22 July 2016